Ziefert

FOR ERROL F. MARGOLIN
A.K.A. BUZZY

Text copyright © 2004 by Harriet Ziefert
Illustrations copyright © 2004 by Emily Bolam
All rights reserved / CIP Data is available.
Published in the United States 2004 by
🍎 Blue Apple Books
515 Valley Street, Maplewood, N.J. 07040
www.blueapplebooks.com
Distributed in the U.S. by Chronicle Books
Printed in China
ISBN: 1-59354-069-8

A LIFT-THE-FLAP STORY

SOMETIMES BUZZY SHARES

HARRIET ZIEFERT   **EMILY BOLAM**

Blue Apple Books

Buzzy has a play date
with two school friends.

"Let's play dress-up," says Buzzy.

"Okay," says Allie. "I'll be a king."

"And I'll be a ballerina," says Sally.

"Let's ride bikes," says Allie.
"Buzzy can ride the red one.
And I'll ride the blue one."

"But what can Sally ride?"

"She can ride
the wagon."

Then Sally wants to ride a bike.
But Allie says, "No . . . it's still my turn."

It's not fair!

Buzzy's mother hears the noise.
"What's happening?" she asks.

Buzzy and Allie don't answer.
Sally says, "They won't share!"

"Give Sally a turn, then come inside for a snack."

"Here are six cookies, two for each of you. Do you want juice or milk to drink?"

Then Sally and Allie
want to play with the toys
in Buzzy's room.

"It's time for you-know-what,"
says Buzzy's mother.

"Do we have to clean up?"

"You do."

"I like the way you put everything away!" says Buzzy's mother.

"Good-bye, Sally. Good-bye, Allie."

"See you later,
alligator!"